One TV Blasting
and a Pig Outdoors

Deborah Abbott and Henry Kisor

Illustrated by Leslie Morrill

Albert Whitman & Company, Morton Grove, Illinois

The text of this book is set in Stone Serif.
The illustrations are rendered in watercolor.
Design by Lucy Smith.

Library of Congress Cataloging-in-Publication Data

Abbott, Deborah.
One TV blasting and a pig outdoors / by Deborah Abbott and Henry Kisor;
illustrated by Leslie Morrill.
        p.   cm.
Summary: Conan describes life with his father
who lost his hearing at the age of three.
ISBN 0-8075-6075-8
[1. Fathers and sons—Fiction. 2. Deaf—Fiction.
3. Physically handicapped—Fiction.]
I. Kisor, Henry. II. Morrill, Leslie H., ill. III. Title.
IV. Title: One television blasting and a pig outdoors.
PZ7.A1460n 1994
[Fic]—dc20
                                                           94-6649
                                                           CIP
                                                           AC

For Tina. *D.A. & H.K.*

To all those in publishing,
without whom the book illustrator
could not survive—my heartfelt thanks. *L.M.*

B EEP, BEEP, BEEP," announces my alarm clock. My favorite music blares from my radio.

"Conan, honey, time to rise and shine!" my mom calls.

Stanley, our dog, jumps off my bed and peers out the window. A deep, throaty growl erupts as he spots his Labrador friend, Cody, on his morning walk with his master.

I wait until I hear my brother, Colin, turn off the shower; then I head for the bathroom.

After a quick breakfast, I dash out the door. "Don't forget your lunch," Dad reminds me.

Halfway to school, my best friend, Adam, yells from behind me, "Wait up, Conan! I can't walk that fast this early."

In school, the clanging of lockers echoes through the halls. I skip into my classroom just as the bell rings. As I slip behind my desk, the public address system blares, "Good morning, students. Our special assembly celebrating Martin Luther King, Jr.'s, birthday begins at 9:00 sharp. Teachers, please bring your students to the auditorium at 8:55."

As we enter the auditorium, the school band is playing. The program begins with everyone reciting the Pledge of Allegiance. Then we listen to a recording of the "I Have a Dream" speech by Martin Luther King, Jr. We finish by singing "We Shall Overcome."

This is what my morning is like: full of sound, of noise and chatter. What would it be like never to hear any of the ordinary sounds we take for granted? What would it be like to live in a world of silence? No alarm clock. No radio. No songs or pianos or guitars. No shouted reminders from my parents. No sounds from my dog. No hails from unseen friends. No announcements from the school PA system. No famous voices from our past.

It would be a very different world.

It is my dad's world.

My dad is deaf.

My father hasn't heard a sound since he was three years old, when a disease called meningitis destroyed his hearing.

My dad talks. But he sounds different from other people. His voice is breathy and monotonous, almost like a foghorn heard through the mist and wind from far away at sea. He sounds that way because he can't hear himself talk.

"It's like drawing a picture with your eyes shut," he says. "You can't watch where the pencil goes. The picture isn't as skillfully drawn as it would be if you could see it while you drew it."

But you can understand what Dad says, especially if you stop to listen.

Sometimes I can't hear him over the noise of other things, such as a passing truck. Because he can't hear the truck, he doesn't know he must raise his voice so I can hear him. I have to say, "Dad, a loud truck went by. What did you say?"

My dad reads lips. He can understand what most people are saying if they speak slowly enough and look right at him. If they turn their backs to him, he is lost.

Sometimes he has trouble understanding strangers. When that happens, he will ask someone he can understand to tell him what the other person has said. If there is nobody around, Dad will simply ask the other person to repeat and repeat until Dad gets it right.

If he still can't understand, Dad will pull out pencil and paper and ask the other person to write down the message. This does not happen very often, though. And it almost never happens with people Dad knows, because he's used to their ways of speaking.

Lipreading is not easy because so many sounds look alike. Did someone say "hat" or "cat"? The other words in a sentence often help Dad tell the difference. If the person says, "Put the hat on your head," Dad will know nobody's talking about a cat.

Sometimes Dad makes huge mistakes, and they can be funny. One day when Colin was little, he ran into the living room from the kitchen and said to Dad, "What's that big loud noise?"

Dad got up from the couch and peered out the window with a puzzled expression. "What pig outdoors?" he asked.

"What's that big loud noise?" and "What's that pig outdoors?" look almost exactly alike when you say them. Try saying these questions in front of a mirror without making a sound, and you'll see.

Colin and I learned to lipread, too, because we are around Dad so much and just picked it up by watching his lips as he spoke. We tease Mom by talking to each other at the dinner table without using our voices. Dad knows what we say, but Mom can't understand. (Lipreading is a knack. Some people pick it up easily, and some don't.) Sometimes she thinks we are planning to play a trick on her. But we aren't talking about her at all!

I also have fun lipreading across the room at school, if my target isn't too far away. I mouth the words silently and then lipread what my friend says back to me. The teachers don't like it any more than Mom does.

Many deaf people use sign language, but Dad doesn't know how to sign. When he was growing up, there weren't any other deaf children in the little town where he lived. He had to learn to speak so that he could have friends and go to school. To do this, he took speech lessons.

He still does. He has to practice his speech so people can understand him. He makes up these crazy sentences with all the sounds he needs to practice. For example, he sometimes needs to make his "e" sounds a little sharper. We'll find him sitting at the dining room table saying over and over, "Evil babies eat eels by the seashore."

My father says he's like a baseball pitcher who needs to throw every day to keep his skills sharp. "If I don't practice," he says, "I'll have trouble getting my words in the 'strike zone' where people can understand them easily."

My dad is a newspaper editor and columnist, and he writes books, too. He makes speeches and appears on television and radio shows. He says the speech lessons really pay off. They are hard work, but worth the effort.

Sometimes someone asks why he doesn't learn sign language. He says it's because he has to take speech lessons in order to do his job well, and right now he doesn't have time to do both. He might learn someday, though.

Many people believe deaf children should learn sign language first, then learn to speak. Other people feel that it is more important for deaf children to learn to speak first. Deaf people themselves disagree about this.

Dad says he thinks the choice is a difficult one. He is glad his parents chose the path of speech and lipreading for him, but he will support whatever choice the parents of deaf children make.

"It's like religion," he says. "People disagree about the best way to worship. But we don't judge people by the church they choose, do we?"

One problem, Dad says, is that deaf people are not all the same. Some are born without hearing. Others lose their hearing in early childhood, as he did. Still others become deaf as adults, many as they grow old. There are different kinds of deafness, too. Some people, like Dad, are profoundly deaf, which means without usable hearing. Some are severely deaf, others are slightly deaf. Some people can hear low sounds but not high ones. Some can hear better with hearing aids, some cannot. Some grow up with sign language while others grow up with spoken language. Many learn both speech and sign language.

People use different words to describe their hearing loss, or lack of hearing. Many people use "hearing-impaired" as an overall term for any kind of hearing loss.

Others who speak sign language are very proud of it and do not think that their ears are "impaired" at all. They call themselves Deaf people, with a capital *D*.

Still others prefer the term "hard-of-hearing." Many of these people can hear with hearing aids.

"I can't hear at all," says Dad. "I am deaf."

"We're all different," he adds, "and our needs are different. Making the right choices to take care of our needs is more important than the labels we use to describe ourselves."

11

Dad often tells us stories about what it was like to be deaf when he was little.

Right after he lost his hearing, he had a very hard time. Meningitis, an infection of the membranes that cover the brain, not only made him deaf, but paralyzed him temporarily and caused him to lose his sense of balance.

The high fever of meningitis apparently affected his brain's ability to tell his arms and legs what to do, but the paralysis wore off after a few weeks. His balance organs, which are part of the ears, were damaged by the fever, too. To this day, Dad cannot walk in a straight line with his eyes shut. He needs to have a horizon to focus upon. His eyes have taken over for his ears in more ways than one.

Soon my father also forgot how to talk, because he couldn't hear himself or anyone else. He didn't understand that he had to move his lips and make sounds with his voice box so that other people could hear the words he was thinking.

He quickly learned to lipread simple things like "ball" and "throw." But anything more complicated was impossible for him to understand.

One day Dad wanted some chewing gum. (He liked it so much he remembered how to say the word "gum"!) His mother didn't have any, and neither did the store. This was during World War II, and there was a shortage of chewing gum. My grandmother had to drive him to the store to show him the empty chewing-gum shelves.

How did Dad learn to speak? He already could talk when he

became deaf, and although for a while he forgot how, the memory of speaking never quite left him. His mother and father—my Nana and Granddad—found a special teacher of the deaf. This teacher believed in teaching deaf children to speak by first teaching them how to read. She believed parents should be the teachers, and she taught them how to teach their children.

Every day Nana sat down with Dad at a little table to teach him how to read. At some point, Dad says, he made the connection between word and thing. He does not remember how it happened, but he says it must have been very much like the famous moment in which Helen Keller, the deaf and blind philosopher and writer, learned that the word "water" meant the cold fluid that was being poured over her hand from the backyard pump. The dam of silence burst, and the magic of language washed over young Helen.

"For me, the floodgates of memory must have opened at that moment, too," Dad once said. "I must suddenly have remembered what it was like to talk."

I once asked my father whether it was a printed word or a spoken word that allowed him to make the connection. "I just don't know," he replied. "It happened so long ago, when I was very young. I think learning that a word printed on paper stood for an object, like an apple, reminded me that a certain sound made with the mouth also stood for the same thing."

In the beginning, Dad had to learn all over again how individual sounds were made. "Ap-puh," he would say when he saw the piece of fruit. He had a hard time remembering the "l" sound, and Nana had to show him, with the help of a mirror, how to place the tip of his tongue behind his teeth to say "apple."

When Dad's friends, who could hear, saw that Dad was learning to read, they asked Nana to teach them, too. Some days Dad's house looked like a preschool, with all his little friends learning as Nana gave reading lessons to everyone.

Soon Nana brought home books from the library. Every evening Nana or Granddad would sit down with Dad, but they did not read to him, like most parents. He read to them. For him, it was both reading practice and speech practice. But he says he didn't think of it as practice. A new book each evening meant a new adventure, and that was how he grew to love reading.

When Dad was very young, he started reading "The Night before Christmas" to Nana, Granddad, and his brother, my Uncle Buck, every Christmas Eve. He kept on reading that wonderful poem each year, and he was still reading by the tree in Nana and Granddad's living room on Christmas Eve when he was twenty-one years old.

Now, every Christmas Eve we still hear, in Dad's familiar, funny voice, "' 'Twas the night before Christmas / And all through the house / Not a creature was stirring / Not even a mouse . . . '" I bet he'll still be reciting it when *he* is a granddad.

My father says he grew to love reading not just because every story carried him into a new world, but also because it helped him learn things he missed because he couldn't hear. For example, he might not understand a teacher explaining how an automobile engine works, because that's a complicated process, and if he missed one part, he'd miss the whole thing. But a book could

provide him with a complete explanation.

There weren't any schools for the deaf in the small town where Dad grew up. But because Dad was reading already, the principal of the regular school said he could try kindergarten there. If he learned, he could stay in the school.

Dad learned, and he continued attending regular schools. If he couldn't understand the teacher, he would ask for extra reading, and that always helped him fill the gaps in his learning.

He was shy about his speech, which he knew sounded odd.

"I had more ways of ducking out of giving an oral report than a zebra has stripes," Dad told me with a laugh. "I would always mysteriously come down with the flu on the morning I was to speak before a class."

He managed to graduate from high school without giving a single speech. Not until he was much older and had become well known in his community did he discover that people were interested in what he had to say, not how he said it. Only then did he lose his fear of speaking in public. "I grew up," Dad says simply, "and now I give speeches all the time."

When he was still young, other kids liked and respected Dad because he was a good reader and a good athlete, and that made them want to get to know him. He often helped his hearing friends with their reading, and he was always one of the first picked for teams.

He became a good swimmer and in high school was on the swimming team that won the state championship. How did he know when to start? Sometimes, but not often, he could feel the crack of the starter's pistol. "And I just kept my eye on the hand of the swimmer next to me," he said. "When I saw it move, off I'd go."

"Being good at something helped make up for speaking funny," he once told me. "It made people respect me." And when people got to know Dad, they and he had very little trouble talking to one another. He could read their lips easily, and they could understand his speech without difficulty.

There were a few misunderstandings, but sometimes they made everyone laugh, even Dad. One day, walking home from school with a friend, my father sneezed loudly. The friend turned to Dad and said something. "What?" said Dad. The friend said the word again. "What?" Dad asked again.

After repeating the word two more times, Dad's friend took a piece of chalk out of his pocket and wrote on the sidewalk:

KAYZOONHITE

Dad took one look and bent double from laughing. He took the chalk from his friend and wrote underneath the word:

GESUNDHEIT

"No wonder I couldn't understand!" Dad told his friend. "You couldn't spell it right!"

Then it was his friend's turn to laugh.

>━┼━◆━◦━◉━◦━◆━┼━<

Of course, being a deaf kid wasn't all laughter. Though Dad

could manage pretty well, there were lots of frustrating times. When he was a camper and later a counselor at a YMCA summer camp, he says, he didn't especially enjoy the campfires at night.

"Everyone would tell stories and sing songs," he told me. "The fire was never very bright, and I couldn't understand what people were saying because I couldn't see them very well. So I would sit silently, bored out of my mind, until the campfire was over."

Sometimes other people were unfair to Dad. One summer when he was sixteen and on the high school swimming team, he wanted to be a lifeguard at a country club pool. But the directors of the club said no. They didn't want to trust their children's lives to a deaf lifeguard.

The directors didn't understand that hearing isn't always important to a lifeguard. Swimmers in trouble can't cry out because water is choking them. It's their unnatural splashing that attracts a lifeguard's attention. Deaf people are very alert, often more alert than hearing people, to things everybody can see. That's why they can make very good lifeguards.

The same summer, however, Dad was a counselor at the YMCA camp and taught water skiing by himself. The YMCA directors knew what he could do and felt comfortable trusting him with children on the open water.

Some of the campers would try to take advantage of his deafness. In the cabin at night, after "lights out," some boys would still be talking. "After about ten minutes," Dad said, "I'd shout into the darkness, 'Quiet! Go to sleep!' And they'd simmer down. How did I know? The counselors in the nearby cabins told me.

"Of course I didn't know *for sure* they were talking. But I was a kid once. I'd talk with the kid in the next bunk by shining a flashlight on his face so I could read his lips. We all talked after lights out. And so did my campers.

"They never caught on that I really couldn't hear them talking in the dark."

When Dad grew up and went to work, he lived alone in his own apartment. This was before telephones for the hearing-impaired had been invented, so he couldn't call up his friends. He had to go over to their houses and knock on their doors, or write letters to them.

It wasn't easy for him to make dates. If he wrote a letter on Monday, he had to wait until Friday for a reply, and if the young woman said she already had plans, there was nothing for Dad to do that weekend.

"How did you meet Mom?" I asked him one time.

"She was a blind date," he replied. "An old high school friend fixed us up."

"What did you do on your first date?" I asked.

"I took her out to a nightclub," he said. "Unfortunately, I didn't know the nightclub was a very noisy one, with a very loud piano. She couldn't hear me at all, let alone understand a word I said.

"And do you know what? She once told me that before I took her home that evening, she knew she was going to marry me."

"Huh?" I said. "How did she know that?"

"Conan, go figure," he replied. "I have no idea."

Today many deaf people who live alone have hearing-ear dogs, just as blind people have seeing-eye dogs. Before Dad married Mom, he had a kind of hearing-ear cat, a big yellow tom named Fred.

Whenever someone knocked on the door of his apartment, Dad would be alerted as Fred rushed to the door as if expecting someone with his breakfast.

Fred learned early that meowing hungrily wouldn't wake up Dad. That cat learned to sit on Dad's chest when he was asleep and lick Dad's eyelids with his tongue. "It was like waking up with someone sandpapering my eyes!" Dad said.

But Fred wasn't always helpful. Once he knocked over Dad's alarm clock, which had a flashing light instead of a bell, and made Dad two hours late to work.

>-+-◆>-+-O-+-◆>-+-<

Today Dad uses a "vibrating pager" for the doorbell. A small transmitter with a microphone sits under the doorbell chimes. When the doorbell rings or someone knocks, the transmitter sends radio waves to a receiver Dad wears on his wrist like a watch. The receiver vibrates rapidly, and Dad knows someone is at the door.

Dad can wear the receiver anywhere in the house and even in the backyard, and he'll always know when someone has come to call.

We have a sweet, lolloping half-Labrador, half-Doberman

named Stanley, whom we sometimes call "Mr. Velvet Ears." Just for fun, Mom has tried to train Stanley to go get Dad when the doorbell rings, but Stan just sits, tail wagging, tongue hanging out, panting joyfully. He's eager, but he's not very well trained.

Dad thinks there might be hope for Stanley, though. One morning when Mom was at work, Dad vacuumed the upstairs and then left the vacuum cleaner in the hall. All day Stanley kept following my father around, cocking his head, looking at Dad in an expectant way.

"Stanley," Dad said, "what do you want?" Stanley just sat there, looking perplexed.

After school I ran into the house and found my dad working in his computer room. "Why is the vacuum cleaner running in the hall?" I asked.

"Oh," said Dad, "so that's what Stanley was trying to tell me!"

Maybe Stanley can be trained. We keep working on it. But it doesn't matter, Dad says. As long as hearing people live in the house, there's no need for a "signal dog," one term for a dog trained to help deaf people. We can love Stanley just the way he is.

If my father lived alone, he'd not only get a signal dog but also rig up a flashing light for the telephone so that every time someone called, he would know that the phone was ringing. He has one of those lights at his office for his telephone there.

For a long time my father couldn't use the telephone at all. When I was a baby, Mom and my brother had to tell him what the caller said, then tell the caller what Dad said. But today Dad uses the telephone a lot, although he still can't hear.

One of the machines he uses to "talk" on the phone looks a little like a portable typewriter or a laptop computer. It's called a "TTY," short for "TeleTYpewriter." Other people call it a "TT," for "Text Telephone." (A less commonly used term is "TDD," short for "Telecommunications Device for the Deaf.")

A TTY, TDD, or TT has a keyboard and a small screen. When Dad types on the keyboard, the words appear on his TTY screen and the screen of the TTY belonging to the person he is calling. And the words the other person types appear on the screen of Dad's TTY. Some TTYs are attached to little printers so that the user can reread the conversation on paper after hanging up. What one person types appears in capital letters, and what the other types appears in small letters, so you always know who said what.

Once, before we all went on vacation to Glacier National Park, I watched Dad as he used his TTY to make hotel and train reservations. Mom used to have to make all our travel arrangements, and Dad was very proud that now he could do it, too. "It was an instrument of liberation for me," he says.

Today many hotels, railroads, airlines, stores, and offices have TTYs so that deaf people can do business with them.

Most hearing people, however, don't have TTYs. If the person Dad wants to call doesn't have one, Dad calls the phone number of a voice relay service. He types on his TTY, and the words appear on the TTY of the relay operator, a hearing person. The operator tells the other person by voice what Dad is typing, then types what the other person is saying so that Dad can see it on his TTY.

Most people who keep TTYs at home are deaf or otherwise

hearing-impaired. But many of Dad's hearing friends have a computer with a modem, a device that allows two computer operators to communicate over the telephone lines. Special software on Dad's computer turns it into a "BBS," or "Bulletin Board System," so that his friends can call with their computers at any time and type in messages for Dad or pick up messages from him. Dad can "talk" to them over his telephone line with his computer, too; the messages he and his friends type appear immediately on each other's screens, as if they had TTYs.

When Colin is away at college, he often calls Dad's computer with his computer, and they "talk" together with their keyboards. This is very important to Dad, for sometimes he doesn't see my brother for months.

Some new TTYs can talk with computers as well. Dad uses one of these at work.

There are lots of people who have neither computers nor TTYs, but keep fax machines at home. Dad uses his fax machine to communicate with many of them.

Just the other day, Dad came home with tickets to a baseball game. I couldn't go, so he sent a fax message to a friend: "I've got two upper-deck seats for the Cubs and Reds game tomorrow. Want to go?"

Five minutes later his friend replied with another fax: "Yes! The hot dogs are on me."

With his TTY, computer, and fax machine, Dad uses the telephone so much that Mom, who is a great telephone talker, complains that his long-distance phone bills have grown as big as

hers. And sometimes he hogs both our telephone lines, using one of them to send a fax or talk on the TTY while his computer bulletin board uses the other. She often says to him, "You're just trying to make up for lost time for all those years when you couldn't use the telephone!"

And Dad says, "Right you are!"

When you're watching television, sometimes you see the words "Closed-Captioned for the Hearing-Impaired" on the screen. You can't see the words of "closed" captions on your TV screen unless you have a special decoder to "open" the captions. Today the decoder electronics are built into all TV sets with screens thirteen inches or larger that are sold in the United States.

The closed captions repeat what people on many TV programs or video movies are saying. (Sometimes news shows and children's programs also show a sign language interpreter in a corner of the TV screen.) The captions also tell about sounds, such as music, backfiring cars, or slamming doors, that are important to the hearing-impaired viewer's understanding.

Even some of the commercials on the TV are closed-captioned, so that hearing-impaired people can find out about the new products being advertised and "read" the jingles about breakfast cereals and other products familiar to hearing people.

For a long time Dad couldn't understand what was happening on TV programs. He had to use his imagination, creating make-believe scripts in his head to fit the action on the screen. (Sometimes, he says, when he found out what was really happening on a TV show, he liked his imaginary scripts better!)

Dad doesn't go to the movies anymore. He used to, but now most commercial videos are also closed-captioned. He says, "Why should I go to a movie that I can't understand when I can wait a few months and see it on the VCR and catch the whole plot?"

A few years ago, after watching many closed-captioned British TV shows, Dad suddenly realized that he was no longer having trouble understanding people from England. The captions had helped him learn to lipread English accents better. (Interestingly, many new immigrants are learning how to read, write, and speak American English with the help of closed-captioned videos.)

Many, but not all, deaf people can "hear" with cochlear implants. To insert a cochlear implant, a surgeon places a tiny button called a "receiver" under the skin behind the deaf person's ear. A thin wire runs from the button into the cochlea, the part of the ear that sends sounds to the brain.

A computerized "processor" the size of a pack of cards is worn on the body, sometimes on the chest and sometimes on a belt. The processor picks up sounds from a microphone, "processes" them with its computer, and transmits the sounds to the receiver behind the ear.

With the implant, some people who have been completely deaf can "hear" well enough to talk on the telephone, to hear birds singing, and even to enjoy music.

Dad investigated the cochlear implant for himself, but discovered that the meningitis that destroyed his hearing when he was a child had also changed his cochlea so much that a surgeon would not be able to get enough of the wire into it to allow Dad to hear most sounds.

"It doesn't really matter," Dad says. "I already have a happy life and can get along very well without the implant. Yes, I would like to hear music and the voices of my family, and talk on the telephone as other people do. I know what I am missing. But I enjoy so many other things in life that I just don't spend much time wishing for what cannot be.

"All the same, maybe someday the cochlear implant will be improved enough so that it'll work with ears like mine."

⊱┈✦┈◯┈✦┈⊰

All these wonderful electronic advances have made my father's life, and the lives of deaf people all over the world, much easier. But there are times when no fancy gadget is going to prevent the trouble Dad's deafness can cause. The difficulty almost always happens while he is traveling.

Sometimes my father runs into a little problem on the train he takes home from work. If the train is late, holding up all the trains behind it, the conductor may announce on the intercom that the train will not make its last few stops but will go right to the end of the line. All passengers for the last few stops are to get off the train and take the next one a few minutes behind.

Of course, Dad doesn't hear the announcement and doesn't get off the train. And, just as he gets up from his seat, the train zooms right past his stop.

Fortunately, the end of the line is not very far from his stop, and within a few minutes Dad can catch another train going in the opposite direction. It doesn't really make him very late, so he says he can live with the annoyance.

"For me deafness is an irritation," Dad says, "not a disaster. Often hearing people think being deaf must be a terrible thing, because they can't imagine what it is like not to hear. They don't realize that people can learn how to cope with silence, to make up for the lack of hearing. And they don't understand that coping with deafness can lead to interesting adventures—sometimes more interesting than I'd like, of course!"

Once Dad was traveling to Boston on an airplane. Because of bad weather in Boston, the captain announced that the plane would land in Hartford, Connecticut, instead, and the passengers would be sent on by bus to Boston.

Naturally, Dad did not hear the announcement, and when he got off the plane he said to himself, "This isn't Boston! I've been to Boston many times, and its airport sure doesn't look like this one!"

Luckily, a flight attendant on his plane had gotten off behind Dad, so Dad turned and asked him, "What's going on here?"

Hearing Dad's "deaf speech," the flight attendant quickly understood what had happened and told Dad where to find the bus for Boston. It was a long trip, but Dad was happy to get to his destination without further confusion.

Sometimes the "adventures" occur while other people are traveling. Once Dad went to the airport to pick up my brother, who was coming home from college. But Colin had taken an

earlier flight and arrived an hour before the plane he had told Dad to meet. Dad couldn't hear a voice message, so Colin couldn't have him paged at the airport to tell him he was already there.

He went to the gate where the later plane was to arrive and looked for Dad. He couldn't find him. So he sat down to wait. Time went by, and Dad didn't come. That is not like him, my brother thought. Our father always arrives at the airport in plenty of time.

When the later plane taxied up to the gate and my brother still did not see Dad, he started to worry. Just as the ticket agent walked by to open the door to the gate, Dad suddenly stood up next to an enormous potted plant that was right beside my brother. He had been there all the time, and Colin could not see him because he and Dad were sitting on opposite sides of the plant, which blocked their views.

My brother reached forward and tapped him on the shoulder. "Hi, Dad," he said.

My father whirled around in surprise. "How did you get off the plane so fast?" he said.

Colin hugged him and started laughing.

➤━┥◄➤━O━◄➤┝━◄

A lot of people ask me what it's like to have a deaf father, how it's different from having a hearing father. That's a hard question for me to answer, because I've had only one father!

But I really think that it's mostly like having a hearing father, only a little bit different.

For example, I can't call "Dad!" and expect him to answer. I have to go find him and place myself where he can see my hand as I give a little wave or touch him on the arm. He will look up and say "Yes?"

Some people think this is a lot of trouble, but I don't think so. I've been doing it all my life. I can remember being two or three years old and riding in the child's seat on Dad's bike. I learned very early that if I wanted to talk to him when we were out on the bike, I had to pat him on the back so that he would stop the bike and turn around to look at me. You get used to the little things you have to do when you live with a deaf father.

Dad always goes to our school programs, just like other fathers. He always takes a book with him and sneaks in a little reading while the other grades are performing. When it's my grade's turn, he'll watch us intently, smiling and clapping with the other parents. Of course, he can't hear a thing, but he wants to be there for me, like other fathers.

Some people think Dad must depend on me, my brother, and my mom to be his ears. That's not true at all. Once in a while Dad will ask me to make a short phone call for him if it's faster than using the TTY relay service, or if there isn't a TTY around. Or if Dad doesn't understand someone, he'll look at me quickly for a translation. But that doesn't happen very often, for Dad is a stubborn guy and always wants to do things himself.

Many of my friends are nervous about talking to Dad. They

worry that he won't understand them, or that they won't understand him, and both they and Dad will be embarrassed about it. This makes Dad laugh because he always manages to communicate with just about anybody. But it makes him sad, too, because there are lots of people he'd love to know, but they're afraid to talk to him.

So how do you talk to Dad? Talk to him as you would to anybody else's father. Just make sure he's looking at you, and speak distinctly. When he talks to you, listen carefully. That's all you need to do—Dad will take care of the rest.

Really, life with a deaf father is just like life with a hearing father—except, for Dad, there's no sound at all. And that can make life with him very interesting.

Mom likes to tell a story about something that happened one morning during the Christmas holidays, when Colin and I were small. She had just walked into the living room where Dad was talking to a friend. She couldn't hear a word he said, and neither could Dad's friend, because all of a sudden things had started to happen.

The siren at the fire station in the next block was screaming out its weekly test. Somebody had arrived at the door, so the doorbell was chiming. My brother had the TV on with the volume turned high. I was very little, and had fallen down and begun to cry just

as the telephone rang and the oven timer went off.

And my father chattered on, utterly unaware of all the noise.

To this day Mom says she can't listen to "The Twelve Days of Christmas" without thinking,

> *One siren screaming,*
> *one doorbell chiming,*
> *one telephone ringing,*
> *one child crying,*
> *one oven buzzing,*
> *one TV blasting,*
>
> *And a pig outdoors!*

Then she laughs. So do my brother and I. And so does Dad.

American Sign Language (ASL)

A language employed by deaf Americans and English-speaking Canadians, using the hands, body, and facial expressions. The order in which words and ideas are signed in ASL is different from the order used in spoken English.

Assistive devices

Special mechanical or electronic devices that help deaf and hearing-impaired people. For example, a "vibrating pager" is a tiny machine worn on the wrist that picks up radio signals from a small transmitter mounted on a door or placed next to a telephone. When someone rings the doorbell or knocks on the door or when the telephone rings, the transmitter sends a radio signal that causes the pager to shake vigorously.

Another assistive device is a special alarm clock that flashes a light or shakes a bed to awaken a sleeper. An amplifier is available to make telephone voices louder for hard-of-hearing people. Special flashing smoke alarms warn hearing-impaired people about fires. Still other devices help them "talk" on the telephone. (See TTY, TT, TDD.)

Auditory-verbal Communication

A way of teaching hearing-impaired children to speak and understand English by training them to rely on what hearing they do have, with the help of hearing aids.

Bulletin Board System (BBS)

A computer system that allows people with a computer and modem to dial in over telephone lines and send messages to other BBS users. People can also read messages left for them. It is like a computer mailbox. On some BBS systems, people can also "talk" directly with other users by typing words that appear on each other's screens. Many hearing-impaired people communicate with others this way.

Closed-captioning

A way in which printed captions appear on the screen of a TV set. The captions repeat what people say on a television program or video. Captions also tell if there is music or other sounds that help a hearing-impaired viewer to understand the program. Captions are visible only if a decoder is attached to the television set or built into it. Today decoders are built into all television sets with a screen thirteen inches or larger sold in the United States.

Cochlear implant

A computerized "artificial ear" that helps some people to "hear" sound again or for the first time. After much training, a person may be able to recognize some sounds as words. A doctor inserts a tiny wire into the "cochlea" (KOHK lee uh), a part of the inner ear. The wire leads out to a small round "receiver," which the surgeon plants just under the skin behind the ear. A special box, worn on the body or belt, called a "processor" picks up sounds and sends them to the receiver over an electric wire.

Cued speech

A method of communication in which speakers use "cues," or special hand movements, to help lip readers distinguish among sounds that look alike on the lips.

Deaf, deafness

Being partially or completely unable to hear. Professionals often use the term "deaf" to describe people who cannot use their hearing, with or without an aid, to communicate. The term "hard-of-hearing" is often used for people who *can* use their hearing, with or without an aid. "Hearing-impaired" is sometimes used as the general term to indicate all people with any degree of hearing loss. This book uses "hearing-impaired" in that way. (See hearing-impaired.)

Deaf culture

The history and accomplishments of deaf people, including sign language, fingerspelling, American Sign Language Poetry, Story Telling in American Sign Language, and art that includes aspects of deafness. Many people, particularly those born deaf, take great pride in deaf culture and tend to socialize mainly among themselves. They often refer to themselves as "Deaf," spelled with a capital *D*.

Deaf-mute, deaf-and-dumb

Old-fashioned terms that mean "deaf and unable to speak." Because deaf people can speak in sign language if they cannot speak with their voices, these terms are now considered out-of-date as well as hurtful, and should be avoided.

Fingerspelling

A kind of sign language in which every letter of a word is spelled out with hand shapes. People who use sign language often use fingerspelling to communicate a name or a word for which there is no sign.

Hard-of-hearing

A term used to describe people who have enough hearing, with or without a hearing aid, to be able to understand speech.

Hearing aid

A device that makes sounds louder so that a hearing-impaired person can hear them. Some are very tiny and are worn entirely in the ear. Some hearing aids are built into glasses.

Hearing-ear dog

Also called a "signal" dog. A dog specially trained to tell its owner about sounds. For example, when there is a knock at the door, the dog will touch its owner and run to the door to show where the sound is coming from. These dogs are taught at special schools, and like guide dogs for the blind, they can go anywhere their owners go, such as restaurants, airplanes, and trains.

Hearing-impaired

Another term for "deaf" or "hard-of-hearing." Many deaf people do not use this word to describe themselves or others with hearing loss. They believe that there is nothing wrong with being deaf, and that they are not impaired in any way, just different.

Lipreading

Understanding what is being said by watching the movements of the mouth of the person who is speaking. Also called "speech-reading."

Oral communication

Communication by speaking, listening with or without hearing aids, and reading lips.

Pidgin Sign English

A sign language that uses fingerspelling and the signs of American Sign Language, but not the grammar. Pidgin uses the word order of spoken English.

Relay service

A special telephone service in which a telephone operator helps communication between hearing-impaired and hearing people. The operator receives a voice message from the hearing person and transmits it via TTY to a hearing-impaired person, or receives a TTY message from the hearing-impaired person which is relayed by voice to the hearing person. (See TTY, TT, TDD.)

Sign language

A way of communicating words, ideas, and feelings using the body, especially the hands, arms, and face. There are many different kinds of sign language. In the United States and English-speaking Canada, American Sign Language, Signed English, Pidgin Sign English, and fingerspelling are the most common forms of sign language. (See also American Sign Language, Signed English, Pidgin Sign English, and fingerspelling.)

Signed English

A kind of sign language in which the words and grammar are very much like those of spoken English. Words are signed in the same order as they appear in spoken or printed English sentences.

Simultaneous communication

Talking with another person by using spoken words and sign language at the same time.

Total communication

Talking to another person by using all possible ways of communicating: speech, listening, lipreading, sign language, fingerspelling, pantomime, and writing.

TTY, TT, TDD

A machine with a keyboard like a typewriter and also a small screen that allows the user to "type" words over the telephone to another person with a similar machine. The person receiving the words reads them on the screen and then types back. Some people call the machine a "TTY" for "TeleTYpewriter." Others use "TT," for "Text Telephone." Some people still use "TDD," for "Telecommunications Device for the Deaf." "TDD" is seldom used today, because hearing people who cannot speak often use this machine.

Deborah Abbott is a school librarian and a reviewer of children's books for newspapers and magazines.

Henry Kisor is a newspaper writer and editor. He is the author of two books for adults, *What's That Pig Outdoors? A Memoir of Deafness* and *Zephyr: Tracking a Dream Across America.*

Deborah and Henry have two grown sons, Colin and Conan, and live in Evanston, Illinois, with their dog, Stanley.

Leslie Morrill is a father, teacher, and student. He is a native of Hudson, New Hampshire, and now lives in Washington, D.C., with his elegant wife and daughter. He has illustrated many books and hopes to illustrate many more.

All of the events related in this book are true. Some of them also appear in *What's That Pig Outdoors? A Memoir of Deafness.*